UNDEAD IN VEGAS

STEPHEN ALEXANDER NORTH

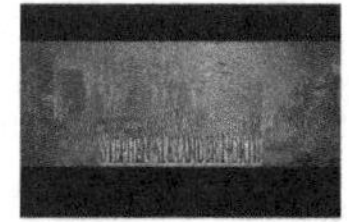

Stephen Alexander North

Dr. Pus, Michael West, read a fragment of this story on his podcast several years ago.
I'd like to dedicate this story to the dream he built back in 2008 and to all the good librarians.
Proud to be part of all that, but mourn the passing of The Library of the Living Dead/The Twisted Library.
Doc, you are missed.

Praise for Undead in Vegas

"As I was reading, I could hear the amusement park ride announcer: *Passengers, please fasten your seat belts. Remain seated and keep your hands and feet inside the ride at all times. Avoid all contact with those outside the ride until Undead in Vegas by Stephen Alexander North comes to a complete stop!* It's crazy wild ride and at the end I wanted more." Kerri C Gregory

"Zombie Vegas." -Patrick D'Orazio, author of Comes The Dark

"A pleasant surprise. I picked up Undead in Vegas, not really expecting much, and for some reason quickly became absorbed by it." -Wally World

"Lots of action. North throws readers across a highway and straight into zombie hell." Astradaemon's Lair

"Fun Dead Read. I love Stephen North's zombie fiction. For me they just work as pure escapist fun. Love tat he doesn't take himself too seriously. Gordon Wallace is a cool character. And while no novel is perfect, I had no problem giving this zom romp five stars." -J. Sousa

"I wasn't expecting that ending at all." Ophelia Kee

(Author: in response to Ophelia Kee) "Me either."

Character Description by Ophelia Kee

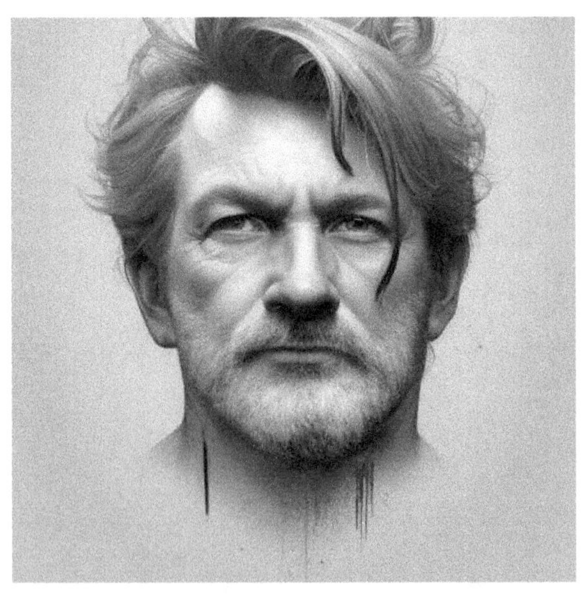

Wallace Gordon is a middle-aged divorced guy. He needed a new life after his bitch ex-wife got the house, most of the money, and all of his friends. Driving a big rig was a quick fix for a midlife career change. It took less than six weeks to obtain the necessary license and start over the road trucking, leaving the past as far behind him as it was possible to do. It wasn't far enough.

At fifty-two, Wallace is facing the effects of a broken loveless marriage. He's overweight, has indigestion, possible encroaching alcoholism, and erectile dysfunction. He wasn't looking for love and no woman was looking for Wallace Gordon.

As Undead in Vegas begins, Wallace is riding a rig with almost as many issues as he has. He's the new guy, even as an older man, he's taking his lumps as he attempts to rise in the commercial trucking industry. He's almost arrived at his destination. Only he never quite makes it.

Book Description

What's dead in Vegas, doesn't always stay dead in Vegas! The zombie apocalypse has begun, but not everyone is immediately aware of what's happening. As the situation escalates and more of the country is affected, people are scrambling to secure their positions by whatever means may be necessary.

Wallace Gordon is another divorced guy heading to Vegas to drown his sorrows when he gets trapped in a traffic jam, his rig blows up, and he gets bit by a possibly zombified hooker. And that's just the beginning of his troubles...

Undead in Vegas is a short story set in the world of the Dead Tide series and is an apocalyptic thriller horror tale. Grab your copy now and join Wallace for a fast-paced, in-your-face, deadly dangerous thrill ride.

CONTENTS

BEYOND APOCALYPSE

If you enjoy apocalyptic horror, thrillers, and science fiction tales, you will love Stephen Alexander North's prose fiction. Subscribe to his **Beyond Apocalypse Newsletter** to get the latest news, updates on book releases, free stuff, and more.

Undead in Vegas

Dawn is breaking on an ugly day in May when I run into heavy traffic. I'm hung over, and the inside of my truck cab smells like the Italian Sub I ate last night. High time to air things out and roll down my windows for a few minutes. Reminds me that there's a terrible story behind me, but I'll save you the details. The bare bones of my past are that I'm fifty-two, about forty pounds overweight, and sometimes need a little medicinal help after being in a loveless marriage for years.

So, where does this leave me, you might ask? On the road. In the months following my divorce, I went to a truck driving school to get a Commercial Driver's license. Been driving a company rig on my own for a month and a half now.

At the moment, I'm almost at my destination. Seen some crazy traffic the last few hours, and

I'm wondering what's going on. My in-dash radio quit working, and I don't have a CB. The low man gets the beat-up piece of junk, I guess. Cheap bastard owner. I could check my cell phone, but I'm focusing on driving. I see the exit sign, then an overturned car, a police cruiser, and a bunch of cars piled together just as I take an exit ramp off Interstate 15 for Las Vegas. See an oil slick covering the road, try to slow down, clip the rear of another semi-trailer and run up and over the police cruiser. My rig careens across two lanes, overturns onto the driver's side and slides into the guardrail. I'm thrown around like a doll, but my seat belt saves me.

My heart's pounding and hands are trembling as I unfasten my seat belt and climb up and out of the cab, through the passenger side. The truck's on fire, so I jump off and down to the road. People are running around, screaming and shouting for help. Someone in a Hummer drives through the crowd without stopping, and several people get run over. Something explodes not far away, and I duck the bark of a large caliber revolver. I spot a cop holding a gun. She's struggling with two people and losing the fight. I hear her scream and run her way. I have to do something. Her gun skitters across the pavement toward me. One attacker rips out her throat with his teeth, while the other gnaws an arm.

What the fuck?

I might be in zombie hell.

Smoke billows across the road, probably from my truck, and a hulking man with an axe runs through it. I scoop up the revolver and watch as the crazy guy chops both of the cannibals...and the cop!

The axe-man's face is a gory mess. His hair is stringy with sweat, and plastered to his forehead. While the bodies are still twitching, he wipes his face with a shirt sleeve, then cleans the axe blade off on the cop's pant leg. I see him squint over at me, teeth bared in a grimace as he hefts the axe.

I raise the gun. I'm guessing five bullets left, because I only heard one shot, but who knows what I've missed already?

"Yah!" the axe-maniac screams.

I squeeze the trigger, and the gun belches fire and thunder. I miss at less than ten feet with my first shot. The guy doesn't even blink or break stride as he raises the axe on high.

My second shot hits him in the gut and ruins his day. His legs give out and crumple beneath him. My ears are ringing, and I can barely hear his screams.

He curls up into a fetal position, bleeding out between his fingers, as I leave him lying there. I make my way down the exit ramp. I stop beside a car at the edge of a parking lot.

With a large percussive thump, my tanker truck blows up, and strews a flaming sheet of debris. An angry cloud of smoke billows toward heaven: Hardly how I envisioned entering Sin City. Nothing seems to go my way. Some moments are better than others. Probably sums up a Vegas vacation as well as any. Hiding outside behind a beat-up Chevy Citation in the furnace-heat of the Excalibur Casino's parking lot doesn't fall into the better moment category. Feel feverish and thirsty as I kneel behind the car and try to catch my breath.

No time to rest, though. The cannibals, or zombies, are everywhere. I have to find some place to hide.

My skin is dry and no longer sweating as I run the last few steps across the soft asphalt. Squint as morning sunlight reflects off the mirrored panels of the nearby Luxor Pyramid. The doors to the Excalibur casino are open and shattered. Pretty dark in there, but hesitating will get me killed. Glass crunches beneath my loafers as I hurry inside. I hold the gun in both hands, aiming everywhere I look, like they do in the movies.

I pause a moment, and open the cylinder on the revolver: Three bullets left. The lady cop doesn't need it anymore, but I do.

The power is off, or someone turned off all the lights and machines. It's quiet as a tomb inside, and smelling like death. The dim outline of a service counter is to my left. In front of the counter there's the body of a scantily clad woman on the floor. She's facedown, wearing a red mini-dress and thigh high boots. Blood cakes the back of her head in her long blonde hair. I step closer, pull out my cell phone, and turn on the flashlight. Inadvertently kick a plastic cup. Gambling chips and the cup skitter across the floor. I freeze in place.

The woman's head moves. Stirred into action by the noise? Hunger? She lifts her left arm, then her right, braces herself and pushes up off the floor. I follow her with the light. See blood on the counter behind her, splashes of red daubed on the carpet.

"Are you okay?"

The words are out of my mouth before I can stop them. If she isn't okay, I have three chances...three bullets, to rectify that. Wish there were more. Wish I grabbed that axe now.

The woman turns toward me, sways on her feet, tottering on spiked heels. My finger is tense on the trigger.

She looked good up until she faced me. A normal person would have blinked from my light, but her eyes are cloudy swirls of red and white. Her mouth, oh Jesus, her mouth, is a twisted snarl of swollen pink gums and blackened kernels that might be teeth...

I pull the trigger. Fire once more as she charges across the short stretch of floor. She crashes into me. Stagger backwards. Feel her hair beneath my chin. Feel that mouth, the dried out chapped lips closing over my throat. The pinch of her teeth tearing my flesh, part of me torn away like an orange peel, and gone forever as I press the barrel between her eyes and fire the last bullet.

The fucking bitch bit me.

Her body slumps to the floor. "You'll be okay now," I tell her through gritted teeth. I stagger forward, dropping the gun. Press my right hand against the wound on my neck as I lean against the service counter. Fuck, it hurts! Have to push past that, and think. Point the cell phone's light at the counter. There's a monthly day planner, a stack of credit receipts, a cup full of pens and a yellow note pad.

Not sure how long I have before turning into one of those things. I should be dead, right? Does it happen right away? Probably won't be long until

I'm just another mindless, shambling dumb fuck looking for my next meal. Ha, I am that already, but maybe I got the one in a million wound. I'm not a zombie yet. Maybe I'll live through this. I pick up a pen, pull the pad toward me, and begin to write:

"My name's Wallace Gordon. I may not live long enough to finish this, but here's my story. I was driving my rig on Interstate 15..."

Story over, right? Really? No way I'm going to try to write all that bullshit down. Got to stop this bleeding first. Need another weapon, too. I'm probably fucking dead, but I'm not going to stand around and wait for it. I go around the service counter. Almost always a first aid kit for emergencies kept handy behind service counters. Spot the white box with a red cross almost immediately. Pull open the plastic snap. Its well stocked: bandages: burn cream; Tylenol; antiseptic ointment; gauze; and peroxide.

Someone told me not long ago that peroxide isn't really good to use on wounds. I've never had the chance to ask anyone if that's true, but it's always seemed to work for me before. I pour half the bottle on my neck, and spread it around. My hands are grubby with all sorts of filth, but I don't have time to find a bathroom. I fight back a scream as the stuff washes across the raw wound and it bites and bubbles.

I give it a few seconds before blotting at the wound with a cocktail napkin, then coat it with antiseptic. Afterwards, I put on a gauze pad and a couple bandages. I think the bleeding's stopped. Nothing major to worry about: I'm going to be fine. Not everything is just like the movies. Feel a little weak, and my neck is throbbing, but I'm still good to go. I'm almost more grossed out thinking about her biting me with that mouth full of rotting teeth, than the thought that maybe she's turned me into a zombie.

Have to quit thinking about it. Nothing I can do now. Besides, the bar can't be too far away. I can get liquored up, and get a room somewhere upstairs with a view. I'm not going to let this slow me down. With twenty-two years of marriage down the drain, no house to live in, and most of my money gone, I'm already a desperate character. I'd planned on a hard-lived vacation anyway by raising hell in Vegas for a week, and then who knows? Am I really going to drive trucks for a living? Talk about strange turns...

I'm in a bad way. This trip was supposed to take my mind of things. Instead, here I stand, mind swirling along in a mad, hopeless dance. I check my phone's battery and it's still got 74% power. I'll keep using the phone's flashlight for now. I notice a purse lying on the floor not far away. Big ass thing. Maybe the bitch has some good shit in there. Maybe some good drugs if I'm lucky. I pick it up, glance through the contents. There's a wallet, a hair brush, a couple tampons, a cell phone, an open pack of 305 cigarettes, a lighter, an unopened pack of 305's cigarettes, and a knife. I wonder if she has a room?

I pull the knifc out. It has a three inch blade, but also doubles as brass knuckles. Not bad. Wish it were another gun, but I'll make do. At least this weapon won't make a lot of noise. I take everything else in the purse, except the tampons, and stuff them in my pockets.

Now, about a room---that thought reminds me that the power's out. Won't be getting into any room with or without one of those electronic keys. But wait, that can't be: The locks have to be battery-powered, too many problems otherwise. I'm betting I'm right. Only problem would be not being able to find someone who already has a key. I take another moment to see if there's a key in the wallet. There is. Sometimes things go my way.

The next step is getting something to eat. Need to find a flashlight soon, before my phone dies.

Wonder if there's any kind of universal key for this place behind the desk? I spend a few more minutes poking around but find nothing useful. Time to keep moving. I hold the phone up with my left hand, and the knife in my right. I enter a broad hall way, pass a door that reads "Authorized Employees Only" and pause a moment before a vast space. See a stretch of carpet decorated in a poker chips pattern, and glimpse the shape of tables and shadowy machines.

Not sure what I expected to see. The only light comes from red emergency lighting, and it isn't enough to illuminate much. I know this is a huge room. I lose my nerve. Back in the hall way I passed a door to a staircase. I'll just see what's in the lady's hotel room. I have an almost overpowering urge to find someplace to hide. Oh God, I'm alone and those things are here somewhere. Everybody's dead. Last live people I saw were up on the interstate, and they were dying fast.

Probably should have tried to help them. Can't handle it: People are eating people out there; in here. My hands are shaking like they do after I've used the weed whacker for an hour, and here I stand paralyzed in a hallway. I hear something crash out in the casino, and turn off the cell phone's flashlight.

I strain to hear more. Hear someone breathing heavy. Not a zombie then. They don't breathe. Right?

"Who's there?" I ask. My words are swallowed up by the darkness, the hush.

"Tell me who you are first?" a woman's raspy voice says. I catch the sharp odors of tobacco and old sweat. Take a step backwards. Then another, and turn back the way I came, running now.

"Wait, please don't leave me!" she shouts.

I stop.

"Please, I've hurt my back and can't get up!" Her voice is hoarse with pain.

It would be so easy to just walk away. I'd be out of range of her voice in moments. Can't escape her words, though. They'll follow me wherever I go, especially if I do the shitty thing and leave her.

"I'm coming," I say, "quit shouting before they hear you."

I turn the phone light back on, and find her behind the next row of slot machines.

She's laying on her back, wearing white slacks, a white button up top and white sneakers. My first thought is nurse, or a maid. Her long black hair is loose, and her mouth twisted with pain. Pretty face, might be Polynesian.

The shirtless corpse of a fat man lies beside her with a broken broom stick sticking in his right eye. Matted wiry black hair covers the fish-white blob from front to back and from shoulders to his ham like fists.

I can only imagine the woman's horror as I kneel beside her.

She reaches for my hand.

"Please get me out of here."

"Take it easy, lady, I'll help you," I reply. "Can you move?"

"It hurts. I hit my back on that machine as I struggled with that thing! I can move if you help me. I'm a nurse, and I think it may just be sprained. Hurts like hell, though."

"You sure?"

"We can't stay here! I have a room on the second floor. Can you carry me there?"

She can't weigh more than a hundred and twenty pounds. "No problem. Let's take your weapon with us, just in case. I stand up, grab the broom handle, and put a foot on the guy's neck. I yank on it, and turn it twice before it comes free along with a lot of gore. I wipe it off on his pants, and hand it to her. I pause a moment.

"I'll hold your phone, too, so we can see," she says.

"Okay," I answer as I stoop, and slide one hand beneath her knees and the other under her left arm and behind her shoulders. "Ready...?"

I lift before she answers, and she screams into my chest. Moans and shuffling footsteps come from deeper within the casino.

At least she isn't the source of body odor and cigarettes I smelt earlier. Quick as I can, I make my way back to the hall, then the door to the staircase. Wonder briefly what it'd be like to be trapped in an elevator when the power went out. No one's coming for you. Feel light-headed going up. I'm not moving with vigor. We come out onto a carpeted hallway. Dim, red light illuminates small, elegant signs that point the way for various room numbers.

"Right," she tells me. "Go right. Room 231."

She's fumbling in her purse as I run.

"Here's my key," she says as I stop in front of her room.

I take the key, a plastic card, and run it through the scanner. A little green light comes on and I'm able to open the door. A strong odor of cigarettes wafts over me as I help her inside. A man's voice asks, "Where the hell have you been?"

The woman, I still don't know her name, answers, "You passed out, what do you care?"

"You should've woke me up!" he snarls.

He's a tall, thin guy with lank blond hair to his shoulders, and a soul patch below his lip. He looks about my age, fifty, or a little older, and is wearing blue jeans, a white t-shirt, a faded blue jeans jacket, and biker boots. He smokes a cigarette that's tucked between his fingers rather than held. A pair of sunglasses are on top of his head.

"Yeah, waking you up always works out well for me when you're hung over!" she declares while easing herself into a padded chair.

"So, who's this?" he asks without looking at me. He has a New York accent, and a raspy voice. His eyes haven't left her since we came in.

"Just a guy who rescued me," she replies.

"Why don't I believe you?"

He still hasn't asked her if she's okay. Has he really been up here while the world went to hell?

"When do you ever believe me?"

"Hey," I say, "maybe I should go..."

He holds up a hand. "Wait a minute, pal. So what did he rescue you from?"

"Look," I snarl, "I don't have time for this. All I did was help the lady up to her room. She doesn't even know my name."

He turns toward me now, and I see that his eyes are a washed out blue.

"So you say. Well, know this, pal, I keep a tight leash on her. Thanks for helping. Now you can buzz off."

"You do know what's going on out there, right?" I ask, instead of saying what I want to say.

Out of the corner of my eye I see the woman reach for a bottle on the table by her chair. She's pulls a Solo cup out of a plastic sleeve, uncaps the bottle and starts pouring. Bacardi Gold. She adds a splash of Pepsi.

"We need ice, babe," he says to her. "More cigarettes, too."

She takes a long swallow, then smacks her lips. "Power's out. Didn't you notice, Ted? Power's out, dead people are walking around, and I'm hurt. You're worried about ice and fucking cigs?"

"What do you mean, zombies or something?"

No mention of her back being hurt. Asshole.

"Exactly what I mean, Teddy, fucking zombies. A fat guy was trying to eat me, and he saved me." She turns toward me. "I'm Ann, by the way. What's your name?"

"Wallace Gordon. Call me Wallace."

She grins, "Not Wally, huh?"

"No."

"Well, Wally," says Ted, "looks like you've been bit, or something. Time to hit the road."

I take two quick steps and stop with my nose inches from Ted's. "I'm having a little trouble with my patience and some anger issues, Ted. Might be best to mind your manners around me. Are we clear?"

He doesn't flinch. A smirk plays at the edges of his mouth.

"Sure. I get you. But we have a little problem here. You've been bit. You're going to turn into one of those things. So that means you need to leave. I don't want to deal with that, not unless you want to go out in the hall, and I'll put you down now. Really don't want to make a mess in here."

"Maybe I won't. This isn't the movies, Ted! Maybe not everyone gets it!"

"He's right!" Ann shouts. "We don't know for sure that a bite affects everyone! We need to wait and see, Teddy. He saved me, after all."

Ted looks exasperated. "Fine, kitten, but he stays away from you. You used your free card on Tuesday."

Free card? Awareness dawns. I look over at Ann, and she's blushing with her eyes downcast. *What happens in Vegas...*

I clear my throat. "Look, none of this is my business. Maybe I should go."

"No, she's right," Ted says, locking eyes with me. "We'll wait and see. Maybe we can help each other. First sign that you're turning, though---you got to go. Understood?"

I nod, thinking: *First chance I get maybe you'll go, pal.*

"Bring me my painkillers, will you please, Ted," Ann asks.

Ted looks away, and goes into the bathroom. He walks with a limp, favoring his right foot. Comes out holding a travel kit and puts it on the table in front of Ann.

"Tylenol's probably not going to touch back pain like that," Ted remarks.

"Anything's better than nothing," Ann replies. "Maybe you two can find a pharmacy and get me something stronger."

I put my hand in my pocket. "Here's a pack of cigarettes, anyway."

"Will you go with my husband to get something stronger?"

I have no desire to go back out anywhere, but we'd need other things soon anyway. Might as well do it now.

"Yeah, I'll help," I say.

"I didn't say anything about going anywhere," Ted says.

"You won't?" Ann asks.

"'I don't want to."

This is getting to be too much. I don't owe these people anything. Ted is a piece of work. If Ann didn't appear to be a decent person, I'd just do a fast fade.

Ted looks up and sees my face. He holds up a hand.

"Look man, I'm not the heroic type. I'll pay you to do it, though."

I shake my head. What's he going to pay me with? It's the fucking apocalypse.

"I'll see what I can find, Ann. Hang in there."

I hear her voice as I open the door say, "Thank you, Wallace. Be careful."

The hallway is lit only by emergency lights. I see a puddle of blood on the carpet a few feet to my right. There's a gory chunk of something in the puddle.

Be careful, eh?

Glad the stairway is the opposite direction.

I take the stairs like an old man, slowly and one step at a time. Should find a place to hide and get some rest. What happens then, though? I either wake up or turn while I'm sleep. No sense worrying.

What happens in Vegas are things I wasn't expecting. How am I going to find a pharmacy without the internet? Wait...maybe that still works even if the phone lines don't! I pull my phone out and hit the Google icon. Notice I'm down to sixty percent power. It doesn't connect. I put the phone away and finish descending the stairs. There's a fire exit at the bottom. The alarm's going to go off if I use it. I notice a fire extinguisher mounted on the wall. There's a lock box on the door. I heft the extinguisher and slam it down on the box. Takes two tries. Things are powered by batteries. I push open the door, hoping nothing on the other side heard me. See a dimly lit service corridor beyond. A red arrow points to the right and at the end of the corridor another fire exit door with a stairway symbol. There's two more doors further down, one on either side. The left one says *Restricted Access* and has a card reader and the right *Security: Authorized Personnel Only.*

The stairwell is an empty space full of echoes. My footsteps make a lot of noise even though I take my time. My headache and neck are still throbbing. Need a long drink of cold water. Just thinking about it makes me thirstier. Lonely, hurting and thirsty. Sounds like a country song. Gives me a few more goals beyond helping Ann. Not much else though.

Can't believe I've come all this way trying to have a little fun, and I'm actually worse off than I was at home. Might even be one of these undead fucks soon. Can't think about that.

I make it to the first floor, and hesitate a moment before opening the door. I pull the brass knuckle knife and fit my fingers into it with the knife blade projecting downwards. I'll probably try to punch my way out of any trouble.

I tell myself there won't be trouble and push the door open.

Someone is standing right there in the hall, half turned away. It's a guy in a security guard uniform. There's a gun in his hand when he turns toward me.

I wait. He's not a zombie.

He has a bad comb-over, and a gut that pushes his belt over.

"Who're you?" he asks. New Jersey accent. The gun is pointed my way.

"My name's Wallace. What's yours?"

"Well, hello there Wally. My name's Clayton Graziano. What are you doing here?"

"Don't call me that. I'm looking for a pharmacy, Clay."

"In a casino's restricted area?"

I count to two and answer, "No, not here. Know of one nearby?"

"Well, yeah. Why?"

"Someone's hurt and needs painkillers."

"A guest of the hotel?"

I count to three. "Yeah. Does that make a difference somehow?"

Clay shrugs, and frowns. "It's been a bad day, Wal...lace, a real bad day. I'm still on shift for five hours. My supervisor won't like it that your back here. Anyway, there's a CVS over a few blocks down South Las Vegas. That's the next intersection east of us down Tropicana. Just go out this exit."

He's still on-shift? I watch him holster his weapon, a revolver of some type. He reaches into his shirt pocket and pulls out a pair of glasses. Then he fishes what looks like a pair of white panties out of his pants pocket. He shrugs at me again, and begins to polish his glasses. Not panties then, but one of those non-abrasive cloths. "Got oily skin. Seems like they're always smudged."

"Is your supervisor around?"

"She's on her lunch break. Something else you need?"

"Nah, but thanks. I need to get moving."

"Sure thing, Wallace."

Ah, progress. I walk down the hallway, open the door and step outside. The door closes behind me and the furnace heat envelopes me again. Only then do I realize he didn't tell me whether to take a left or a right on South Las Vegas. I see some kind of service road, a parking lot on the other side, and then the eastbound lanes of Tropicana Avenue.

A car's coming from my right on the service road. It's a red Suburu Outback. The hood is trailing smoke. The window tint is too dark to see inside, but it doesn't slow down for me anyway. I see a few figures staggering around to my left. Zombies or drunks---who knows.

For the moment, there's nothing moving to my right. Wish I had some sunglasses. Hear gunshots, and screams as I run. Unfortunately from the direction I'm running toward. See a limo halfway up on a curb. The doors are all open. I pause at the back right door and look inside. Nobody there but there's blood on the upholstery of one of the seats, and the liquor bar is full.

The temptation is too much. I'm in pain, and may not be alive much longer. Why am I out risking my life for a stranger? Her life isn't even in danger. Always trying to be the white knight. What good has it done me, and how good am I really? Too many questions! None of them that should be answered while sober and in pain. I step into the back and look at the bottles. See several that are tolerable choices, and then my eyes light on an amber-colored bottle: Evan Williams Honey Whiskey. The seal isn't even broken! Stuff is great without a mixer. I ease back onto a seat without blood stains, and twist the cap off. Lift the bottle to my lips and take a few slow swallows. It goes down smooth.

Hear a helicopter.

I cap the bottle. Better to wait for later. I climb back out, bottle in one hand, and brass knuckles in the other. Can't see the helicopter, but its somewhere close. Cross over into the parking lot. It's almost full. Means a lot of people are still here---somewhere. The big sign for the Excalibur Hotel/Casino looms over me, casting a shadow. I cut between two SUVs and see someone's feet sticking out from behind a Winnebago. The feet are wearing flat-soled women's sneakers and no socks.

Have to keep going. Can't keep stopping like this. Not even to check on that woman. Better not to know what's wrong. Most people out there would have to find out, but I'm not one of them.

Who am I kidding? I step carefully around the RV and see that is a woman, middle-aged, neck-length sandy brown hair, wearing checkered Capri pants and a beige t-shirt. Her purse is on the ground beside her.

She's snoring.

The RV's door is open. A set of keys dangles from the door lock. I'm guessing she is drunk and passed out. She's still wearing shades.

I take the keys, step over the woman, and step up into the RV. "Anybody here?" I ask.

No one answers. Lots of empty space inside. I'm standing in a small kitchen with a dining table booth. Forward of that are two couches, one against either wall, then the driver and passenger seats. To the rear are three doors. Probably a closet back there, a bathroom and a bedroom. Nothing stirs, and the air feels hot and dead. Sweat rolls down my face. I put my brass knuckles and Jack Daniels bottle on the table and go back outside.

The woman hasn't moved. I kneel down next to her. Give her shoulder a small shake. She's out. I make a snap decision and grab her purse, roll her onto her side, get an arm beneath her neck and the other beneath her knees. I lift her up and cradle her to my chest and carry her inside the RV. I lay her on the left side couch. I make sure she's on her side so there's no worry of her choking on vomit. She has a pretty oval face. Can't see her eyes.

I lock the door, but open some windows. Guess it won't hurt anything to wait for her to wake up. I'm assuming this is her vehicle. For lack of anything better to do I check out the rest of the vehicle.

First door on the left is a closet with a bunch of woman's clothing, dresses, high-heeled shoes and purses. The door on the right is a small bathroom complete with sink, shower and toilet. The rear door has a bed and some bookshelves. I'm amused to see that there are a bunch of zombie books. Maybe that shouldn't amuse me.

Have the sudden thought to check whether she's been bit. I hurry back down the short hallway, and the woman is standing up. She has my brass knuckles on her right hand with the blade pointed toward me.

"Back off buster! What are you doing in here?"

Her voice has a nasal Texas twang. Her sunglasses are pushed up on her head, and her eyes are red. The knife hand is trembling.

"Just checking to make sure none of those things are in here. I found you passed out in the parking lot..."

"Save it. I don't know you. Best if you just move on."

I raise my hands. "Hey, watch it lady. No need to swing that at me."

She frowns. "I'll gut you if you don't get out! Where's my car keys?"

"In my pocket. Can I get them out?"

"If you move very slowly."

I reach into my pocket and pull the keys out. "Here you go."

"Throw them on the table."

I toss the keys onto the table and they land next to my bottle of whiskey.

"Were you planning to take my RV?"

"No, I was just trying to help you."

Her frown deepens.

"Looks like you're hurt bad. What happened to your neck?" she asks.

I debate lying to her. "I got bit."

She backs away. "Sorry to hear that mister. I wasn't going to let you stay anyway, though. Best you get going on your way now."

No point in arguing. "Can I have my knife and bottle?"

"Take the bottle. I have plenty of booze."

"I'm dead without that knife."

"I'm sorry, mister. Thanks for saving me, but I can't give you the knife back."

I could probably take it from her.

Instead I grab the bottle, and back toward the door. Feel for the handle.

"Goodbye mister."

"Goodbye."

I turn the handle and step out. Close the door behind me. Hear her lock it. I stand there a moment, and uncap the bottle. Take a few more swallows and feel it start to hit me. Once the whiskey's all gone I can hit someone over the head with the bottle, but not until it's all gone.

My feet carry me away. Not quite a conscious thing, but I need to keep going. Long as I have a purpose...At the edge of Tropicana Avenue I lean down and put the mostly full bottle on the curb. My insides are lit up, but I'm steady. About a half block down I can see a crosswalk bridge linking the Excalibur with the New York New York complex, and beyond that the intersection of Tropicana and South Las Vegas. There's an immense pile-up at the intersection and a fire is spreading. Oily smoke rises in the sky. Looks like there's already been a big explosion. Some people are upright and walking around, but burned bodies are all over. Body parts also.

Four of the figures lurch toward me as I pass under the crosswalk.

All I have is the empty revolver shoved into the back of my pants. Pistol whipping zombies doesn't sound like a good idea. I can run, though. I decide to take a left on South Las Vegas. Wish I knew whether it is the right choice for the CVS. The four are following me, but even my pitiful excuse for a sprint is a lot faster than a shamble. There are five lanes going east and five lanes going west on Tropicana and what looks like a lot more on South Las Vegas. I skirt the leftmost lane on Vegas, and see the Statue of Liberty to my left. There's also a staircase ahead of me on the sidewalk. Don't want to go up there. I dodge in and out between cars. The backup is immense. In one, I see a family cowering as I run past. They're in a big truck with the windows cracked. Not sure why they're there. The woman in the passenger seat looks at me with big eyes while her husband waves a pocket knife at me. I keep going. See other people walking around, but I don't stop or give them more than a passing glance. Breathing hard now. I'm no jogger. I'm down to half a pack of cigarettes a day, but my legs feel like lead and my hearts pounding out of my chest again. Not the kind of Las Vegas action I was anticipating. See a body in front of me. Old guy's still holding a cane with a steel head. He's flat on his back. I skid to a stop and make a grab for the cane. The old guy sits up with a snarl, eyes like white marbles, and his mouth open impossibly wide. My hand closes around the shaft of hickory wood and I raise it high and whip it across his face. His head snaps back and as he collapses back to the pavement I'm back on my feet running again.

More ghouls are coming down the stairs. I climb up onto the hood of a Mazda sedan and slide up and over. Land awkwardly on my feet due to trembling legs. Keep going. Sucking wind. Wheezing.

Hear three rapid fire shots. Don't know where it comes from but its close. Pass under another cross-walk bridge, this one linking New York New York to the MGM Grand. Come to a stop next to a Greyhound bus. As I bend over I see a dead face staring down at me from a bus window. Put my hands on my knees and try to catch my breath. The cane head is a fanged grinning demon. There's dried blood that's flaking away and sticking to my sweaty hand. Doesn't even faze me. Lurch back into a run. See a roller coaster over on the New York side of the street. The elevated tracks ring the complex. See a set of the yellow cars hanging suspended upside down from the red track. People are still in the cars. None of them are moving though and their arms are dangling down. Makes me wonder how long they've been trapped up there.

Keep going, Wallace. Snarls from my right. Push myself hard to pick up the pace. Can't remember whether I took my blood pressure pills this morning. There's a crowd of people on the sidewalk to my right. One or two of them on the fringe see me coming. I cut right in front of a Volkswagon Jetta.

I'm three lanes over running past cars that would be coming at me if they were moving. A young girl with a mouth full of blood and bits of flesh stumbles from between two cars and stops in front of me. I raise the cane high and smash it over the top of her head. She drops, but my feet get tangled and I go down with her. She's too slow to react and I'm able to get back up and step past her. Up again, but thinking about hiding under a car. Anywhere to catch my breath, actually. See an open manhole, but keep going. Pass another bus. See the Shake Shack sign on my left up ahead. Then NYNY's huge sign. Crowds are thicker, closer. There's palm trees in the grassy median to my right. Hear the fronds stir in a slight gust of wind. Cross another jammed up intersection, but I know it's supposed to be one more block. Seeing all the walking corpses raising their arms and turning to follow me is horrifying and hellish. I see feasts taking place, and the remains of feasts. Not one other live person in all this madness. Ahead I see a knot of police cruisers and a van blocking the intersection. Their lights are still flashing and just in front of them are three fallen officers. All three are missing their heads. One has the barrel of a shotgun lying on his chest. Suicide after killing his friends, maybe? It breaks my heart to keep running, but I see the van. There's no time to try to pry a gun from their hands. That van, though. It has to be unlocked. If not I'll run back and hope the shotgun has one last round for me.

Something arcs overhead sizzling and trailing fire. I see the dead turn toward the noise as it impacts somewhere behind me to my left. I keep going. Someone might be trying to help me. I step over the shredded remains of another officer, and then I'm at the sliding door on the passenger side of the police van. Oh dear lord let it be unlocked! My fingers grasp the handle and pull it open. I step up and inside. Pull the door closed behind me. Lock it and the driver's side door. Lower myself to the floor. Hoping I'm alone. I'm too tired to step into the back. Better to catch my breath. Close my eyes. Focus on breathing in and out. Can't stop shaking. Adrenalin or fatigue---I don't know. Both. I've stopped sweating again, and my skin is dry. Aware of a growing headache like a spike through my head. Stomach's cramping. I'm in a bad way, but might be safe.

Put my arm over my eyes. Breathing is evening out. Forehead is hot. Drifting. At some point I fade out.

Wake in darkness. Head is heavy and the headache is still with me. Legs are sore. Not dead though! Remember worrying that I might not wake up. Must be immune. Maybe all I have to worry about is them taking too many bites out of me. Ha. People always want a piece of you. Even in death.

I lever myself up and see the light of the moon through the van's passenger side window. I'm in the swat van. Maybe it's a truck. Whatever. I take a chance and turn on my phone's flashlight app to see in here. There's a doorway behind the two seats to the back. Not sure what I should have expected to see, but what I get is two long bench seats along either wall. There are some storage compartments beneath the benches, but no rows of assault rifles. No weapon lockers. I do see a case of bottled water. I keep to my hands and knees and crawl back there. Keeps me below the sightline of the windows.

I force myself to drink slow. Never been thrilled by bottled water before now. While drinking I look around and find a bunch of first aid supplies in a storage compartment. Only painkiller in there is some Equate Ibruprofen. I swallow five of them. I'm also feeling hungry. Probably pass out again if I keep sitting here. I'm really disappointed that there aren't any guns. Need to keep moving. I crawl back into the cab and poke around. Come up with one of those flashlights that double as a club. Better than nothing. Funny how I don't mind (too much) the thought of punching people, but if they're dead I want some distance. Just for kicks I look to see if the keys are in the ignition. No luck there. Time to look out the windows. I turn off my phone's flashlight and peer outside.

Not much to see without street lights. The moon is full, but its pitch black in the shadows of the buildings. Don't hear anything. I'm not going out there at night. Not even with the flashlight. Better to plan for tomorrow and rest up some more. Try not to think about food. Or what's walking around out there.

Wow. And I didn't think there could be something worse than being in an unhappy marriage.

There's always a new low.

Especially in Vegas, right?

I wake the next morning in stifling heat. I unbutton my jeans, pull my dick out and piss into the two empty bottles from last night. Somehow manage not to make a mess, but why do I care? Then, I drink two more. There's eight bottles left. I'd like to take this water with me. No backpacks to be found in here though. Should have had one of those bugout bags in my truck. Would have been set for this, but then I've always been too much of a pessimist to be a prepper. Living in a metropolis did that to me. I realized that in most situations I wouldn't have enough bullets, or someplace nearby that was safe. Never felt like I had the money to stock up either. Been living on the edge, check to check, for a long time now. That's why this trip had a shadow hanging over it to begin with. There was a load waiting to be picked up here in Vegas, but it wouldn't have paid enough money to save my house. I'd been about to plunge headfirst into the gutter.

None of that matters now. I've won a lottery of sorts in this apocalypse with possibly being immune to this undead virus, or whatever it is. Don't feel lucky, though. Like winning a vacation trip but not having the money to get there. There's always a catch. Sort-of like finding a place to hide but not being able to leave. Hope that isn't the situation I'm in. Better to know. I poke my head up and look around.

Straight ahead through the windshield I can see the three dead cops. I'd really like to get my hands on that shotgun and their pistols. What if they don't have any ammo left? Two people are standing near the bodies. A lot more are walking on the sidewalk on the NYNY side of the street. Too many for me to chance going for the cops weapons. As I sit here I can feel my courage leeching away. Getting bit sucks. Really don't want to be ripped limb from limb. Can't stay here either.

Before I lose my nerve, I grab a bottle of water, the flashlight, open the door, and run north. The crowd to my right lurches into motion, and I wish I was fleet of foot. What's in my favor is that they are clumsy, and trip over one another, but there's a lot of them.

Got a block to go supposedly. Up ahead of me the zombies are spread throughout the cars. Nowhere to go to avoid them. Remember playing football and being big enough to run most people down when they tried to tackle me. That was thirty years ago.

I'm running down a chute really. On either side of me the cars are bumper to bumper. A dead guy is turning toward me in my lane. He was a beefy guy when alive. Right now he looks like a carved side of beef. He's wearing jeans, sneakers and a wife beater t-shirt. The shirt is in shreds and his torso looks like a bloody anatomy dummy. Slabs of ropy muscle and tendon are exposed. He's turning because of the growing roar of the zombies following me. I'm the center of attention. I raise the flashlight high over my head, and focus on where I step. Try to regulate my breathing. There's no room to side-step this guy. Only way is straight through. Four, three, two steps and I swing for his head as he lunges. Feel the heavy head connect as he crashes into me. I slam into the car to my left hard. Feel his arms close around me. See another dead, hungry face right behind him, and swing the flashlight again. His temple gives way beneath the blow and he falls to the ground. I reverse on the backswing and catch the woman behind him a glancing blow across the jaw. Teeth fly and she crumples. I step over him and on her and run. Run past a smart car crushed like an accordion between a Chevy Avalanche and a garbage truck. See movement beneath the garbage truck: A hand waving.

I really don't have time to think or debate decisions. Must be some reason for it. Has to be a live person! I drop down and look. A woman's face. "Crawl under here! Follow me!" she says. I watch her back away and lower herself into an open manhole. I follow.

"Pull the lid closed behind you," the woman's voice says.

I lower my legs into the manhole, and feel for the lid, and pull it down into place behind me. I'm hanging onto a ladder in utter darkness. The air's a lot cooler down here. I turn on the flashlight and point the beam downwards. About five feet down, the woman looks up at me. Her face is smudged and her red hair up in a pony tail. She's still on the good side of thirty wearing a long-sleeved black shirt, yoga pants and sneakers.

I climb the rest of the way down. The floor is dry. Only thing I can smell is me. Getting a little ripe. I'm surprised to be able to stand erect.

"Hi, I'm Joan," she says. "What's your name?" Her voice echoes.

"Hi, I'm Wallace," I reply. "Thanks for helping me."

"Oh, no worries. Say, it looks like you're hurt. Did you get bit on the neck?"

She says that and points a gun at me. Looks like a big-barreled revolver. Big as in .44 magnum big with a kick that'd probably knock her on her ass if she shot me.

How do I answer? If I tell the truth it might freak her out. Looks like she's ready to shoot me. The truth is best, and it is unavoidable. "Yes, but I think I might be immune."

"What makes you say that?"

"Got bit a day ago. You'd think I'd be dead by now."

She lowers the gun and holsters it at her waist. "Maybe not. Well, come on. I'll take you to the others."

"Others? And where is there to go down here?"

"We live down here. Rent's sky high up there, don't you know?"

"Had no idea. I'm from the east coast. Never been here before. Vegas was on my bucket list."

"Your Kick the Bucket list? Guess it's that alright. Follow me, ok?"

I'm surprised how big the tunnel is. Lot of graffiti on the walls, and it's actually bone dry. Some garbage and a smell, but no worse than all the dead people up top.

"Rain's a disaster for us living down here, but we don't get much rain," she says.

I tried to picture all the drains pouring water down here.

"How many of you are there?" I ask.

"Only five and three of us are hardly fit to do anything. Why we need to find more people."

"Makes sense. Only I need to get to a pharmacy near here to help a friend."

"CVS? We can get you close. Where is the friend waiting?"

"She's in the Excalibur."

"Good, that's not far. We should be able to stay underground the whole way."

"You want to help me?"

"Sure. Why not? Maybe you'll stay with us afterwards? Think your friend might want to come?"

"I'm not sure." Truth is, who knows how bad someone wants to live? My ex would never consider living in a trailer home. "I'm guessing her husband might not be too keen on that and we're not really friends. She seemed like a decent person though."

She stops in mid-stride. "She has a husband, and you're the one going to get her medicine?"

"Yeah."

"I shouldn't be surprised. Is he hurt too?"

"Drunken lazy coward is what he is."

She frowns. "Is her injury life threatening?"

"Not if she stays in their hotel room. If she had to run, no way. She's dead then. I don't think she can stand on her own, let alone walk."

"Sounds like she should be in a hospital."

"Yeah," I answer.

"Yeah, guess that's not happening," she answers.

"No, I guess not. I assume this is worldwide? I haven't heard any news reports."

She nods her head. "Maybe some islands are safe. No clue. When it first started happening, it cropped up all over. Some people think terrorists caused it."

"You believe that?"

"Could've been anybody. Doesn't matter now, though."

"Might be something else," I say.

"Okay sunshine," she replies with a smile. "We'll go with that."

"Is now a good time to go to CVS?"

"Yes. We need supplies too. I'm going in with you. Follow me."

She switches on a flashlight of her own and leads the way. I switch mine off, but keep it ready. Anyone nearby could hear us coming. Our footsteps echo, and neither one of us try to talk over the noise. She has an easy athletic stride. My feet and legs ache, mostly due to the running, and my long drive. I tell myself to remember some painkillers for myself. If we're lucky the CVS will be untouched.

I've never been that lucky.

We pass some cross tunnels. Down one of them I see some cardboard boxes and a mattress. A rat skitters away when we get too close. Whenever we stop, the silence closes over us. Too quiet down here. Quick trip though. It is only a matter of minutes and Joan pauses beside ladder rungs inset in the wall.

"This is it," she says. "Only problem, last time I checked there wasn't any vehicle over the manhole.

Those ghouls could be right over us. Not much time to react if they are."

"I'll go first. I'm expendable. Your people need you."

"I won't argue with you, but just take a quick look and lower the lid back down. We don't have to rush this. Good thing is this hole exits almost right in front of the store."

"I'll be careful," I say, and start climbing. When I get to the top I hold on with my left hand and ease the lid up with my right. Right in front of my eyes is the bloody backside of a balding man's head. His wispy hair is matted with gore. Bullet hole I think, but don't look long enough to be sure. No doubt about him being dead and out for the count. Can't see much else unless I shift hands.

"See anything?" Joan calls out softly.

"Just a dead guy," I answer. "I'm going up."

"Okay," she replies.

I slide the cover to the side, and hoist myself out. Joan comes out right behind me. We're in the middle of the street. Right in front of us is the CVS.

Three cars are in the parking lot. I lead the way past them and up to the entrance. The glass doors are shattered. I count ten bodies lying in and outside of the vestibule. They've all been shot in the head. That gives me pause. Is someone inside waiting to shoot everyone that enters, or just zombies trying to enter? Fortunately, Joan pauses when I do.

"What are we waiting for?" she asks.

"Someone shot all these people. Was wondering if we try to go in whether we'll get shot too."

"Let's find out," she replies and steps past me into the store.

A male voice calls out, "Stop right there!"

I'm already following her in, and bump into to her trying to stop.

"What do you want?" the man asks. He's a short dark-skinned guy standing over to the right near the cash register. Two guns are on the counter and another is in his right hand pointing at us.

"We need some medicine and food if possible," Joan answers.

"Hey Andrew, are we sharing?" the man yells.

"I think we can manage that," a voice I assume is Andrew answers. "What kind of medicine?"

"Andrew's the pharmacist," the man offers. "I'm Juan, the cashier."

"We need something for a lady who hurt her back," I answer while walking toward Andrew's voice.

"What happened?" he asks.

I come to the last aisle at the back of the store, and Andrew is behind the pharmacy counter. He's a tall, burly guy with short brown hair. Outdoorsy type wearing a plaid long-sleeve shirt, blue jeans and a gun belted around his waist. There's an open backpack on the counter in front of him.

I answer, "She fell and hurt her back. She told me she's a nurse and thinks its sprained."

"Know if she has any allergies? Pregnant?"

"No idea about allergies. Pretty sure she isn't pregnant."

There's a wall of sectioned shelves behind Andrew. He steps over to the third one over and glances at a few bottles. "Have her try these," he says and hands me a bottle.

I read the label, *"Baclofen."*

"It's a muscle relaxer. There's a few possible side effects like vomiting, dizziness, confusion or drowsiness. Need anything else?"

"I have a terrible headache. Think I got too over-heated yesterday, and stopped sweating."

"You drinking plenty of water?"

"Probably not."

"Drink more then, and Tylenol and Ibruprofin are on aisle six. Help yourself, and take all the water food and drinks you want. Juan and I will be leaving soon. Wife and kids are waiting at my house. Heading for the mountains."

"Best of luck to you, Andrew, and thank you."

"Back atcha, amigo."

I nod, and head for aisle six. Joan meets me there with several reusable bags. "I thought they'd hold up better than plastic ones," she says.

"Maybe we better grab cold medicine along with aspirin and anything else you can think of," I say.

"Yeah, but we need to take more food and drink also. Maybe we can come back later for more."

I nod. We spend the next few minutes in aisle six then move on toward the grocery area. I grab a Pepsi from the cooler and it's still a little cold.

"You should be drinking water or Powerade," Joan says.

"Yeah, I know. Always been addicted to it. I'll fill this bag with the other stuff."

"I love it too. I'm going to see what kind of canned goods I can find."

"See you up front in a couple minutes, then."

"Sure thing," she replies.

I've got an overloaded bag in each hand when I head up front. Wish it were a backpack, but there were none to be had.

"Fuck me!" shouts Juan. The words are followed immediately by gunfire. Each shot a second or so apart as if someone were pausing to aim after each trigger pull. The noise is somewhat muted. Might be a .22. I hear moans and crunching glass.

Juan and Joan appear around the corner as I approach the front. "Back!" Joan says. "We aren't getting out through the front door."

"Tons of them out there!" Juan shouts.

The terror of it is mirrored in each of their faces. I feel panic build within me, but fight to hold it down as I turn to go the other way, back deeper into the small store. A few scattered red emergency lights are on, but the place is dark, full of shadow. The thought occurs to me that maybe four people could hold the front door for a while, but not once the things got in. It's too big in here, and I doubt that these three people have that many bullets. If all the ways out are blocked we're going to die here.

Andrew joins us wearing his backpack, and carrying a shotgun. "I'll trigger the emergency exit on the left and you guys run for the one on the other side. Got it?" he says.

Sounds good in theory, but the alarm is going to attract more of them. No time to argue with him, though.

"I'll meet you at the truck," Juan says.

Andrew hits the other exit, and the alarm blares. He shouts "Not clear on this side!" but even when he slams the door closed the alarm continues. Meanwhile, we reach the other door, not far from the pharmacy, and Juan bursts through it without slowing. He plows right into someone out there and gives a panicked shout. I hear his pistol fire several times before we can join him outside. He's struggling with three people, and more are within feet of us. Shambling figures that lurch into desperate motion. Juan is caught, and already being eaten. A woman has her head buried in his throat, while a man is chewing on his arm. Blood's everywhere. I see Juan fighting to bring the pistol beneath his own chin. The third zombie is struggling to bite through his jeans.

One of the approaching zombies turns toward Joan and I, and I swing the bag with the canned goods against his head, dropping him. I let the bag go, clutch the remaining bag against my chest, and hold the flashlight in my right hand. I bull forward past the fallen zombie and with sadness leave Juan. Joan follows in my wake. There's a lot more zombies between us and the manhole cover. Andrew gives a horrified shout behind us and fires his shotgun twice.

A gray-skinned man in a black suit reaches for me, and I smash the flashlight across his jaw. Teeth fly and he drops away to my left. I drop the remaining bag and grab Joan's hand. I won't leave her behind.

Two more zombies block our way. I turn sideways and kick the knee of the one on the right, plant my foot and smash the horrid thing across the top of his bald head as he falls. There's a sickening crunch, and the impact nearly jars the flashlight out of my hand. The zombie on the left, a willowy brunette woman reaches for me with both hands extended only to be met with one of Joan's bags to the head. The woman drops beside the bald man. Cans spill out, but she holds on to it as we sprint past the fallen bodies.

Andrew catches up to us. "Come with me in the truck if you want," he says. Four more zombies are directly in front of us, but he clears them away with three shots that wreak bloody, horrific carnage. We run past the butchered remains and Andrew double clicks his key fob to unlock the truck: A Ford F150 with a crew cab.

"No, Wallace. Go for the sewer," Joan says, pulling my hand. I don't think twice, but feel bad to see the stricken look on Andrew's face. He isn't going to follow us. We run the past the truck and into the street. I drop to my knees, let go of the flashlight and struggle a moment to lift the cover. Fucker's heavy. I'm still pumped up, though, so the struggle is brief. I heave the steel lid to the side with a clatter, and help Joan down into the hole. More zombies are coming, but I hear the truck engine roar, and Andrew's truck smashes into them as it careens down the street. I lower myself into the dark hole, grab my flashlight and pull the lid back into place.

For a minute or two, I hang there on the rungs, unable to move.

"Did you manage to save anything?" Joan asks.

"All I have is the bottle of muscle relaxers," I answer.

"Not a total loss, then," she replies. "I only lost a few cans."

"Good."

"That was too close. We were lucky."

"Yeah. My legs and arms are trembling."

"Mine too. Can you come down here?"

"Sure," I say, but it takes an effort to move. When I step down, she embraces me. I can feel her shaking. I hug her back.

"I don't want to die that way," she says into my chest.

"No, but this way wouldn't be too bad."

She laughs, then steps back. "We better go. Get that lady her pills."

"Which way do we go?" I ask.

"This way," she says and takes the lead.

I follow her, and gradually my heart beat slows, and my breath evens out.

Seems like a long walk in the dark. Without a watch, I have no real idea. Could've looked at my cell phone, but I'm trying to save the battery. I remember passing smaller branch tunnels, and taking a right turn at a four way junction. We took another right some time later at a second junction.

"After a while down here you have a map in your head," she remarks as we take the second turn.

"Do you know the way out of the city down here?" I ask.

"Sure. If we kept going this way it'll take us under the Interstate and out into the desert. Long walk to get anywhere else though. Pahrump's on the other side of the mountains..."

"Isn't that where Art Bell lived?"

"Who's Art Bell?"

"A late-night radio host. Never mind. We're living a scenario he might have discussed on his show."

"Oh. Outside of the movies, who'd have ever believed this could happen?"

"Lotta people wanted it to happen," I hear myself say.

"I hope my Ex is one of them," Joan says.

"A prepper or a zombie?"

She laughs, "He's a rich guy. I hope he's a zombie."

"Hope mine is too. She's always been a wannabe
rich person."

Joan stops beside a ladder mounted against the
wall. "This should be it."

"Will you wait for me here?" I ask.

"I'll go with you. Never know what you might run
into. Better to be together."

"Thanks, Joan."

"Don't mention it, Wallace."

The manhole cover won't move when I try to lift
it up.

"Must be a car over it," Joan says. "We'll go to the
next one and try it."

I slide the manhole cover to the side and peer
around. The Excalibur is in sight as are thirty or
forty of the dead milling about the parking lot.
They're so spread out it shouldn't be any trouble to
get past them.

"Bunch of them up here, but I think we can make
it inside," I say.

"Let's get this done," she replies.

I climb out and pull her up after me. One thing
sees us and lurches into motion. How do they know
we aren't zombies also? Guess the same way we
can tell they aren't alive. I keep Joan's hand in mine

as we run across the road. She doesn't pull away. More zombies notice us and join in the chase. We dodge around a small pile-up of cars, and almost right into the arms of a large woman wearing a yellow muumuu. Slack, fatty flesh hangs beneath her arms as she reaches for us. We dodge her easily when she steps on her own dress and falls face first to the street.

More close in.: A black man in a blue suit; a brunette soccer mom in sweats; and a Hispanic guy wearing an oversize white t-shirt, checkered shorts and high-top sneakers. The right side of the black man's face is sheared away, including the eye leaving a raw mass of pulped flesh and stark white bone. He's nearly running as he steps in front of me with an open-mouth snarl that separates a piece of tendon. A chunk of bloody tissue flops loose from his jaw to the ground.

I recoil in horror, and smash my flashlight against his face. Horror upon horror: Even with his nose pulverized, he comes on at me. Feel his fingers tangle in my shirt and pull me forward. Stench of death and decay fills my nostrils. Bring my arm up and swing down breaking his grasp. Step backwards. Backhand him with the flashlight. His hands are back on me. Joan's gun roars, but I can't look. She fires again and screams. I lift the flashlight up high and swing down with all my might. The man's head splits wide open, and my fingers go numb and lose their grip. The man goes limp and falls as does my flashlight.

I turn, and see Joan on her back, still screaming as the soccer mom's teeth close around her gun hand. The Hispanic guy is down with a big hole in his forehead. I kick the soccer mom in the face just as her teeth bite through two of Joan's fingers. The mom falls backward and I stomp on her head.

More than necessary, or not, depending on how you look at it.

Joan's no longer screaming, but big tears roll down her face. I realize I'm crying too as I lift her in my arms and make for the Excalibur's fire exit. It's the same one I left by.

"We're both bitten, Wallace," she says.

"Yeah," I answer. "It'll be okay."

Bullshit, but I say it.

"It hurts," she says.

"I know. Hang in there. We'll be safe soon."

"I lost the gun."

"It's okay. I lost the flashlight too."

"Odds are I'm not immune. What will you do when I turn? You should just leave me."

"Shhhh, you didn't leave me, and who says you're not immune. Anyway, we're in this together."

I feel her put her head against my chest. No better feeling than that when you're holding a woman. I hold onto that feeling and cross the parking lot as quick as I can. I see figures closing in from all sides, but focus on making it to the door. If the guard didn't leave it open for me, we're dead anyway.

The moans of the dead grow to a chorus. I shoulder past a zombie with no arms. Stiff arm a slim woman with a bloody scalp and no hair. Reach the door with people grabbing at my shoulder and left arm. Bellow with rage when a beefy guy in a Hawaiian shirt and plaid shorts tries to wrestle Joan away from me while I pull the door open. I pivot, turn and punch him in the jaw with all the torque I can muster. He stumbles backward, rips Joan's shirt, and I take Joan inside. The door opens out, of course, so there is no closing it. We run down the hallway, with the hideous moaning din following hard on our heels.

No sign of Clayton as we go into the stairwell. Joan's crying, and trying to hold her shirt together with her wounded hand. Lot of blood, some of it smeared on her cleavage. She catches me looking, giggles, and says, "Must look like Elvira."

"Much better," I answer. We come out onto the landing for Teddy and Ann's floor, and Clayton is there. He's turned toward us, and it looks like he vomited on himself. There's a big, chunky stain on the front of his security shirt, and gunk in his chest hair. He has a McDonald's bag in one hand, and what might be a squashed Big Mac in the other. I notice his pistol is still in its holster.

He gurgles something, and shuffles a step toward us.

I don't really want to fight him with just my fists, but what else is there?

"Just back down the stairs," Joan whispers, as if worried he'll hear her plan.

I do as she says, and Clayton comes after us. She's probably hoping he'll...Clayton takes one clumsy step forward too many and suddenly plunges head first. I pull Joan to the side and we hug the wall. There's a sickening thud as his head smashes into a concrete step and bursts like a melon. His carcass comes to rest at the bottom of the flight, bag still clutched in one hand.

"I can't believe it," Joan says.

"That he didn't let go of the bag?" I ask.

Joan snorts.

I follow him down, but with more care. I really don't want to touch him or anything on him, but need his gun.

He doesn't move when I pull the gun free of the holster. I put it in the waistband of my pants at the small of my back.

Joan and I go the rest of the way back up and I ease the door open. Nobody is in the hall. There is some garbage piled up outside Teddy and Ann's room. I pound on the door with my fist. A moment later Teddy opens it. He has the revolver in one hand, and is holding the door open with the other.

"Who's this with you, Wally?" he asks.

I push past him, leading Joan by the hand. "A friend. I have medicine for Ann. Where is she?"

"She's in the can."

I have Joan sit down at the table. I take a knee beside her, and examine her hand. There are two ragged stumps, and the bleeding is bad.

"Got any bandages, Ted?"

"What the fuck happened to her, Wally?"

Joan's eyes are full of tears. I make myself wait a moment before I look up at him.

He's got the fucking gun barrel in my face.

"You two both have to go," he says.

I hear myself snarl at him, but he doesn't back off.

Joan's free hand touches my arm.

"Let's just go, Wallace," she says.

"Get the gun out of my face, Ted."

"Suit yourself, but get the hell out of here," he replies. He steps back a pace, but the gun doesn't waver much.

"We got the medicine," I say. Joan and I stand.

"Help me, Teddy!" It's Ann calling to him from the bathroom. "I can't get up."

"Hold on a moment. I'm seeing our guests out," he replies.

"Wallace found medicine?" she asks.

Ted narrows his eyes.

"Yeah, but he didn't bring anything else. His new girlfriend has a bag, though."

"Oh? I hope they brought cigarettes and some food..."

"Leave the bag, bitch," Ted whispers, and gestures with the gun.

There's a lot I could say, but nothing that would matter to this guy.

Joan lowers the bag toward the carpet. Her injured hand is cradled against her chest. Still bleeding, and it means nothing to him. She swings the bag, and I wonder what she's doing. Ted says, "Put it down!"

"Catch!" Joan exclaims, and, next thing I know, the bag sails through the air at Ted. Joan charges him, and the gun goes off. She continues forward, arms outstretched. Another shot. Catch a glimpse of Ted's terrified face, as I too charge.

Ted screams, and goes down with Joan on top of him.

I pile on, going for his gun hand. See Joan's teeth close around Ted's Adam's apple. Her teeth rip, while I yank the gun free, breaking at least one of his fingers in the process. There's a crimson spray from Ted's throat. His body spasms, and he gurgles. Joan goes in for another bite.

I crawl away, and put my back to the wall. Ted goes still. His left foot thumps the floor once. Joan lifts herself off his body, and sits. She is bathed in scarlet. She raises a hand, the uninjured one, to her chest. As it closes over it, I see a wound pouring blood.

She coughs, "I had to do it, Wallace. Couldn't just be a victim anymore."

I don't know what to say, so I nod.

"Shoot me?" she asks.

I look down at the gun in my hand. Looks like it holds five bullets. Ted fired two. Doesn't even matter now that I have the other gun, too.

"Now, Wallace, while I'm still me."

Oh God. Joan is smiling at me. It's the most heartrending smile I've ever seen.

"What's happened?" Ann shouts. "I'm in the tub and can't get up. Please?"

"Please," Joan whispers.

I raise the gun, and aim carefully. If I miss?

Squeeze the trigger. Joan's head jerks with the impact, evidenced by a small hole just left of center of her forehead. I shift aim to Teddy. Shoot him through the head without a blink. Better to be sure. Give him the last bullet too.

Climb to my feet, and leave the now empty gun on the floor. My boot catches a can of lima beans and sends it spinning. The contents of Joan's bag are scattered all over: Cans of peas; green beans; string beans. All vegetables I've hated since I was a kid. I pick up Ann's medicine.

"What's happening?" Ann's voice pleads. "Somebody please tell me!"

I open the door to the bathroom. Ann is huddled in the tub. I see soap suds, a lot of tanned skin, and a pale pink nipple.

"Oh, Wallace, thank God! What happened?"

"We died, Ann. We all died," I answer.

I expect her to scream, but it doesn't happen. A look of resignation settles over her face.

"We did, didn't we?" Her voice is small.

I pull Clayton's gun from my pants, and place it on the counter by the sink. Put Ann's medicine beside it. I take off my shirt, and reach for my belt buckle. Ann's eyes drift downward.

"Is the water still hot?" I ask.

"Yes. Help me up, and let's turn on the shower. We'll get you cleaned up."

I take off my boots, step out of the pants, socks and boxers.

Ann raises an eyebrow, smiles a little, and says, "Woof."

I climb in with her, and help her to her feet. The soap suds run off her body and reveal a lot of smooth skin, hills and valleys. I reach over and turn the shower on. Take the brunt of the cold water until it heats up. Her hands are on my chest.

"Well, mister, got plans for that club? I'm glad to see you too," Ann says as our lips meet.

We're not quite dead, and I haven't used my free card yet. Still, I'm holding a dream in my arms. She might not be perfect, but who is? Not me. We're just two strangers who found each other in Sin City with only a vague idea what's coming next.

"Time for that later," I tell her. "Your medicine is waiting."

"Thank you, Wallace."

"Da nada, Ann."

Sneak Peak at Dead Tide

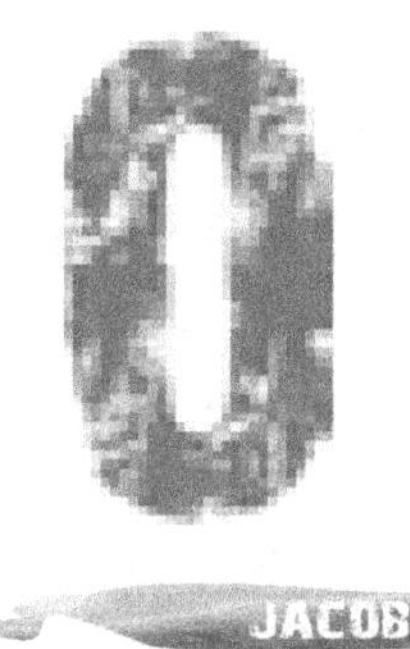

FOR A NUMBER OF REASONS, he finds it difficult to see, but chief among them is the protective mask over his face. Fortunately, it is the newest model, a fairly sleek piece of rubber with large binocular lenses. Even so, he can feel a film of sweat forming on his forehead and cheeks.

As the helicopter drops lower, the haze hanging over the small town becomes apparent. The northern side of the town is enveloped in roiling smoke and flame. The chopper banks right and circles clockwise in toward a parking lot that is the landing zone.

"Get ready, Jacobs," the pilot says over the head-set.

Jacobs takes off the headset and puts his helmet on quickly. The other men around him are already tense and poised, ready to go. The chopper settles, hovering about a foot off the ground, and men jump to the asphalt from the open doors on either side. Jacobs is last, and the chopper is pulling up even as he jumps. He lands fine, and quickly takes a knee, with his M-4 carbine held up to his cheek. He activates the laser sight.

Roughly fifty yards away are a line of storefronts. From left to right they are: a Chinese restaurant, a liquor store, a grocery store, a pawnshop, and a beauty parlour. Some cars off to his left are still parked in orderly rows, but not those near the front of the grocery store. Two cars and a pickup are locked together, burning just ten feet from the store's entrance. Jacobs can smell gasoline. Broken bodies and shattered glass litter the ground. A state trooper's cruiser is parked on the sidewalk at the entrance to a liquor store. No sign of the trooper.

Jacobs glances to his left and activates his mike. "Headcount!"

Each of the five men sound off over the headset. Right now, each is in position, in a circle perimeter with roughly ten meters between each man, all facing outwards to cover each other.

"Listen up. We're going to leapfrog up to the store's entrance. Booth, Hicks, and Lepski will go first. Shell, Watson, and I will follow. Got it?"

"Yes, sir!" "Then move it!"

Shell and Watson move up on either side of him. A second or two later, the other three men sprint toward a camper with a horse trailer. They cover the twenty or so yards without incident. Booth kneels at the rear of the trailer, Hicks at the middle in between the trailer and camper, and Lepski at the front of the camper.

"Go," Jacobs orders, and his men comply, scrambling to follow him as he sprints left of the trailer toward a scorched yellow minivan. Somebody with an automatic weapon opens up, firing several bursts that tear up the asphalt all around him. A shot whines past and another tears a gouge across his right thigh. Breath rasping, he makes the final few steps and falls near the rear of the van. Shell and Watson drop beside him a moment later.

"You hit, Sarge?" Shell asks, leaning over him. He, too, is breathing hard.

"Just creased along the thigh. I'm more pissed off than hurt." "Yeah, who the hell is shooting at us?"

"Not sure, but it sounded like a Thompson."

Watson looks up. "You mean that World War Two submachine gun?"

"Yes. Did either of you see where the shooter was?"

"I think it came from the liquor store, Sarge," Watson answers. "You want me to put some stink on him?" He hefts his light machine gun like a toy.

Jacobs shakes his head and laughs. *Putting some stink* on someone has been the big joke lately. "Be ready in a moment to do just that." He then keys his mike. "Booth, you and the others, be ready to lay down cover fire for me and Shell. We're going to rush the storefront. Think we got a shooter over at the liquor store. Copy? Over."

"Roger," Booth replies. "Whenever you are ready, Sergeant, we are, too. Out."

"Ready Shell? Let's go!"

Gunfire erupts and the tinted glass windows and door of the liquor store shatter. Someone leans around the police cruiser. Before Jacobs can fire, several rounds hit the guy and knock him flat on his back. Jacobs keeps running. The crease stings with every step but is manageable.

Suddenly the fire slacks off, and he and Shell run past the guy near the cruiser. Sure enough, there is a Thompson in his hand, and bullets have literally riddled his body.

Just some crazy fuck trying to stay alive.

His boots crunch on the broken glass as he hits the remains of the door at a sprint.

His boots slip in a big puddle just inside the door, and someone just inside grabs his protective jacket and the suspender for his ammo pouch as he falls backwards. A snarling, snapping nightmare straddles him. The carbine is lost. *Where is Shell?* Can't see, but he has one hand on the thing's throat and the other struggling with its ripping fingers. He can feel his equipment belt coming apart. The thing lunges and his hand on its throat can't stop it. His mask almost comes loose with the impact of the thing's face.

Oh Jesus, it's chewing on my mask!

So weak. No energy to fight much longer.

A shot rings out, deafeningly loud. The weight of the thing falls away.

"Fuck Sarge, I'm sorry, I just couldn't draw my pistol quick enough. I couldn't use the Ronson here, or I'd toasted you both."

"No problem Shell, I think I'm all right. But this mask has to go. I can't see a stinking thing."

"That woman was chewing on it. Probably saved your life."

The suction is too great for a moment, and the rubber resists, but it comes free, bringing almost immediate relief to his sweaty face. Vision returns.

He looks at the mask in his gloved hand. The eye-pieces are smeared with blood that is still dripping.

"You said woman?"

Shell nods. "Yeah, it was a woman all right, and if she wasn't trying to bite your face off, I might've been tempted to leave you two alone." Jacobs lifts an eyebrow. "Don't go there Shell, I'm warning you. Now, where is my carbine?"

"Have a look yourself, Sarge. Look at her…"

Jacobs turns fully toward Shell, and before he can stop himself, grabs the man by the throat. The other man's eyes are wide behind the lenses of his mask. "Get moving, Private! Back outside!"

He gives the man a push backwards.

"Sure thing, Sarge," Shell says over his shoulder.

Once the other man is gone, Jacobs gives in and looks at the body. She is wearing a light green jogging outfit and tennis shoes. Her hair is long, and a light brown with blonde highlights. His rifle is right beside her.

Wonder what her face looks like? What color are her eyes? A distant shout snaps him back.

Why am I looking at a dead woman?

Because there is no chance they'll look back. This one isn't going to recoil in fear, hatred, or disgust. No restraining orders. No shouting or screaming.

No nothing.

He feels a tear course down his cheek, and a long shudder wracks his body.

He picks up the rifle, checks it over, then heads for the exit.

Once outside, he finds his men behind nearby cars, spread out once again in a circle perimeter, covering all approaches.

Shell stands up. "Are we going to clear the buildings, Sarge?"

Jacobs can see most of the others looking over at him, waiting for an answer.

"No, we're not, Shell. You are going to burn them."

"But there may be healthy people still trapped in there. What if some people are still alive? I can't kill innocents."

Jacobs lifts his carbine up a bit, and the red dot of the laser sight plays across the asphalt at Shell's feet. "You heard my order, Shell. I'm getting impatient."

It is impossible to read the man's expression behind the mask, but he nods, then steps forward from behind the cover of the minivan. He aims the nozzle of the flamethrower and slowly squeezes the release and ignition triggers, which requires both hands, one on each pistol grip.

There is a roar as Shell directs a jet of the burning fuel up and onto the roofs of the stores.

They'll thank me later, Jacobs thinks.

PRAISE FOR DEAD TIDE

"A militant zombie novel that. like all good zombie novels, bares the predatory nature of mankind. A wonderfully brutal debut for Library of the Living Dead." – DL Snell, Author of Roses of Blood on Barbwire Vines

"Dead Tide is a fast-paced journey full of zombie mayhem, in which ordinary people encounter the most gruesome monsters, both living and dead. Any fan of zombie fiction should enjoy this page turning romp." – Dr. Kim Paffenroth, Author of Gospel of the Living Dead, Dying to Live, and Dying to Live: Life Sentence.

"Absolutely Brilliant. So well written. I want more!" – Rach Bull

"Saint Petersburg, FL is filled with hungry soulless monsters. Also, zombies." – C.T.

"Brilliant start to this series of books. Great characters and plenty of fast paced scenes..." Kindle Customer

"The zombie apocalypse is here in a fast paced book from Stephen North. Multiple characters try and survive the zombie seige of their town, somehow it all comes to a head in the end. But wait its not the end! The sequel is out already! Great read, interesting characters and end to end action. I am currently working on the next one and its just as good. The most awesome points of Stephen's work is his ability to juggle many, many characters and make them all very unique and the non stop action all coming together for a well paced book. Great stuff!" – Rogzombie

"Dead Tide, buy this book and read it NOW! So I got in this first book from the Library of the Living Dead Press and was instantly delighted at how many pages there were. It's a heavy book to be sure and it is chock full of one of the most powerful zombie novels I have ever read..." – Terrence Patrick Rooney

"The best part is the unpredictable nature of the series. I never knew who was going to live or die, and I never knew what particular obstacles each character would face." – Astradaemon's Lair

Thank You, My Readers

Thank you, sincerely, for taking another chance with one of my stories. I appreciate your support of my work more than you know. When you finish reading if you will leave your kind review, I would enjoy reading your thoughts about my work. Sincerely, -SAN

WANT MORE?

Subscribe to **Beyond Apocalypse** newsletter to receive updates about Stephen Alexander North's writing.

Watch Book Trailers, Vlogs, and other videos on **YouTube**.

Follow Stephen Alexander North on Social Media:

Facebook

Instagram

Pinterest

Twitter

Visit the **Beyond Apocalypse** Blog

For more stories by **Stephen Alexander North**

Thank you for your support of an Independent Author.

Sincerely,
Stephen Alexander North

ALSO BY STEPHEN ALEXANDER NORTH - BEYOND APOCALYPSE

Poetry

I Held the Sun

The Dark Joy for Despair

My Soul's on Fire

Prose

About Author - Stephen Alexander North

Author Bio: Stephen Alexander North is a Florida native, a closet lounge singer, and the obscure Floridian writer of sci-fi, horror, thrillers, fantasy and poetry. He has a Bachelor of Arts in English Literature from the University of South Florida, and served as an Army Reservist.

For More Visit:

Beyond Apocalypse

Books 2 Read